Of Wonder and Dreams

Written and Illustrated by
Leah A. Newton

Of Wonder and Dreams

Published by Leah Newton Books

ISBN-13: 978-0615910062

Dedicated to my daughters
Elise and Sienna

Who show me everyday
the joy and magic in the world.

Do you see the swimming mermaid...

'in a quiet blue lagoon?

And delightful little fairies...

dancing 'neath the golden moon.

Do you see the sleeping dragon...

in a kingdom's far-off land?

And lovely white unicorns...

prancing in the woods so grand?

To find these magical creatures,
you don't need to cross the seas.
Within you there is treasure...

discover these mysteries.

You're more enchanting than the mermaid...

and all the songs she sings.
I hear the laughter in your voice,
it's one of my favorite things.

You're more special than the fairy...

and all the dust she sprinkles.
I see the magic in your eyes,
they're full of little twinkles.

You're more spirited than the dragon...

and all the fire she can breathe.
I feel the glowing in your heart,
it's what helps me to believe.

You are braver than the unicorn...

and all the quests led with her horn.
I've known the marvel of your search,
since the day that you were born.

Stay always full of wonder...

you are what you believe.

Imagine that you shimmer,

we are made...

of WONDER

and DREAMS.

This heartfelt poem reminds us that the enchanting qualities we yearn for in mystical creatures like mermaids, dragons, fairies and unicorns, are in fact already there inside of us. After all, we are all made...of wonder and dreams.

Author and Illustrator: Leah A. Newton

Original Artwork created with acrylic paint on canvas.

Editorial Director and indd Layout: Mary Econome layersdesign@att.net

About the Author

Leah Newton has a Bachelor of Arts in Dance and a Masters in Education, both from Loyola Marymount University in Los Angeles. She has been an educator for 16 years, teaching grades K-12. Leah is a self-taught artist who enjoys working with acrylics on canvas. She finds the medium of children's books a perfect blend of her talents; artist, dancer, storyteller, and teacher. Leah lives in Sacramento, CA with her husband and two daughters.

Find her on www.etsy.com - Leah Newton Prints

www.ingramcontent.com/pod-product-compliance
Lightning Source LLC
Chambersburg PA
CBHW041141010826
48981CB00036BA/435